Mandy [...] with a
very smal[...] called

[S]tella!" and the tiny dog turned round,
s[h]owing Cara and Mum the white patch on
h[e]r tummy.

"She is *so* cute!" Cara squealed. She bent
d[o]wn and put her fingers through the cage.
"Hello, Stella!" she breathed. Stella trotted
[o]ver to sniff Cara's hand, limping slightly on
[h]er front leg.

"She's a Staffie, do you know what that
[m]eans?" Mandy asked Cara. Cara shook her
[h]ead. "A Staffordshire Bull Terrier," Mandy
[e]xplained, opening the door and letting
[M]um and Cara in to see Stella properly.
"They're known for being really courageous
[a]nd loyal dogs." The little puppy looked up
[a]t them and gave a grin, her tiny pink
[t]ongue poking out of her mouth.

Have you read all these books in the **Battersea Dogs &** **Cats Home series?**

STELLA'S
story

by
Sarah Hawkins

RED FOX

BATTERSEA DOGS AND CATS HOME: STELLA'S STORY
A RED FOX BOOK 978 1 849 41414 2

First published in Great Britain by Red Fox,
an imprint of Random House Children's Books
A Random House Group Company

This edition published 2011

1 3 5 7 9 10 8 6 4 2

The Random House Group Limited supports the Forest Stewardship Council
(FSC), the leading international forest certification organization. All our titles
that are printed on Greenpeace-approved FSC-certified paper carry the FSC
logo. Our paper procurement policy can be found at
www.rbooks.co.uk/environment.

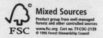

Mixed Sources
Product group from well-managed
forests and other controlled sources
www.fsc.org Cert no. TT-COC-2139
© 1996 Forest Stewardship Council
FSC

Set in 13/20 Stone Informal

Red Fox Books are published by Random House Children's Books,
61–63 Uxbridge Road, London W5 5SA

www.**kids**at**randomhouse**.co.uk
www.**rbooks**.co.uk

Addresses for companies within The Random House Group Limited
can be found at: www.randomhouse.co.uk/offices.htm

THE RANDOM HOUSE GROUP Limited Reg. No. 954009

A CIP catalogue record for this book is available from the British Library.

Turn to page **93** for lots
of information on the
Battersea Dogs & Cats Home,
plus some cool activities!

❧ ❧ ❧ ❧

Meet the stars of the Battersea Dogs & Cats Home series to date . . .

Bailey

Misty

Chester

Rusty

Max

Daisy

Snowy

Stella

A Broken Leg

"But it's sooooooo itchy!" Cara wriggled about on the waiting room seat. Her right leg was resting on the three plastic chairs next to her, covered in a thick cast. She tried scratching the plaster, but it didn't get rid of the tickly feeling on her leg.

"It's not for much longer," Mum said, stroking Cara's dark brown fringe back from her face.

Cara had had her leg in a cast for six weeks, ever since she fell over in the wet playground at school. She had been having a race against her friends Andrea and Natalie when she slipped. She'd landed awkwardly on her leg and when she tried to get up she felt dizzy and sick. Natalie raced to find Mrs Barnes. Mrs Barnes gave Cara some medicine to stop her leg hurting and drove her to hospital where the doctor took a picture, called an X-ray, of the bones in her leg.

It showed her
the little line just
above her ankle
that meant it
was broken.

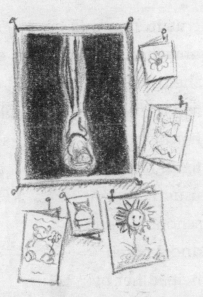

The X-ray
was pinned on
Cara's bedroom
wall now, along
with all the Get
Well Soon cards from her friends. They'd
all admired her cast – especially since it
was bright red! The nice doctor had let
Cara choose the colour when she'd put
the cold plaster round her poorly leg to
hold it nice and straight while it healed.

It had been fun decorating the cast
with signatures and pictures, but Cara
had quickly got cross that she couldn't
use her leg properly. She had to lean on

crutches to walk
anywhere, and
she couldn't
run or play for
her netball
team like she
usually did. At
school Natalie
and Andrea
helped her by
carrying her
books and
opening all the
doors for her, but Cara

hated having to move so slowly. She tried
to bet one of the boys in her class that
she could go faster than him – even on
crutches – but Mrs Barnes had stopped
them and asked Cara if she was trying to
break the other leg too!

The worst thing of all was that Cara hadn't been able to go on holiday with Natalie. Natalie's family was going on a trip to their holiday home at the seaside and they'd invited Cara to go too. Natalie's big brother had promised to teach them how to windsurf, and they were going to go riding at the local stables. Natalie had already told her all about Georgie, the naughty horse she'd ridden there last year. But Cara couldn't do any of that with her leg in plaster.

Cara had been really cross when Mum told her she couldn't go.

"Sweetheart, you can go next year," Mum had said.

"You can't do any of the things you'd planned while your leg is in plaster – and you don't want to spoil Natalie's holiday for her either."

"I can do everything!" Cara had shouted. She used her crutches to hop into her room, and started putting things into her suitcase, pouting stubbornly. Mum followed her in and watched as she made a big mess, pulling her clothes out of her drawers while standing wobbly on her one good leg.

When Cara had turned to throw her swimming costume into her case, she nearly fell over. "Woah!" Mum said, catching her and lowering her down until they were both sitting on the floor.

Cara burst into
tears and Mum
hugged her close
and kissed her
forehead. "You
can't even stand up,
how do you expect to

go windsurfing?" she asked gently. "I've
already spoken to Natalie's mum, and
Andrea's going to go instead of you."

Cara had sobbed even harder. Now
both her best friends would be having fun
without her. "It's not fair!" she cried.

"I know, sweetheart," Mum said. "But
these things happen. You're just going to
have to be brave and try to be pleased that
your friends are going to have a nice trip. I
know they both feel really bad that you
can't go – but you'll be able to go another
time and it'll be just as much fun then."

That evening Cara spoke to Natalie and Andrea on the phone. The disappointment had made a big lump in her throat, but she managed to swallow

it and tell them to have a brilliant time.

"We'll bring you back a present," Natalie promised, and Cara said thank you, making her voice sound cheerful even though she wanted to cry.

"I'm really proud of you," Mum said, when Cara put the phone down. "I know it's not much, but at least you can still have ice cream," she offered, handing Cara a bowl that was filled with her favourite ice cream – mint choc chip. Cara gave her a small smile.

"What are we going to do with you, eh?" Mum sighed, ruffling Cara's hair. "Racing about everywhere, breaking your poor leg! We need to find some way to get rid of all that energy of yours!"

"Well, I do know one way . . ." Cara said in a pleading voice.

"Oh, don't start that again!" Mum replied laughingly.

"But Mum, if we had a puppy I could take her for walks every day, and I'd probably be so worn out I wouldn't even be able to run anywhere."

Mum smiled. Cara continued in a rush, "And you love dogs, and you always say that we can have one one day."

Cara paused. Mum usually stopped her asking about a puppy straight away, but this time she actually seemed to be thinking about it. She tried to think of as many good reasons as she could. "She could guard the house, and walking her would be good exercise, and it would make me feel better, and I have been VERY brave," she added, hopefully. "Please, Mum, please please please!" she cried, running out of ideas.

"OK!"
Mum
burst out.

Cara
dropped
her ice
cream spoon
in surprise.
"OK, what?"
she asked.

"OK, we can get a
dog!" Mum laughed.
"Wasn't that what you
wanted?"

"Yes!" Cara shrieked. "But I never
thought you'd say yes!"

"Well, I am saying yes!" Mum smiled.
"But it'll have to be an older dog, not a
puppy. I don't think I can cope with an
energetic girl *and* an energetic puppy!"

Cara grabbed her mum and squeezed her as hard as she could. She didn't mind if the dog was old or young, as long it was a dog of her very own!

Meeting Stella

Cara jumped as the door opened and
Doctor Sophie poked her head round it.
"Ah, hello, Cara!" she grinned. "Time to
get rid of that pesky cast, eh?" Cara
hopped down and followed her, leaning
on her mum's arm. Mum lifted her up
onto the hospital bed and Doctor Sophie
came over with a funny circular saw.

Cara suddenly felt nervous. What if

the doctor slipped when she was cutting the cast and chopped Cara's leg off? She felt even worse as Doctor Sophie turned the saw on and it made a horrible buzzing noise. "Maybe I'll just keep the cast on . . ." Cara started to say.

Doctor Sophie looked at Cara's scared face and smiled kindly. "It's going to shake your leg a bit," she said, "but I promise that I'll only cut the plaster – not you! We don't want to hurt that leg now that it's all nicely fixed, do we?"

Cara nodded bravely and closed her eyes as the saw whirred on again. As it touched the cast she could feel the shaky vibrations on her leg, but it didn't hurt a bit.

"There we go!" said the
doctor, finally. Cara
looked down and saw
her pop the cast
open like it was
an Easter egg.

"Can I keep
it?" Cara
asked, tracing
the picture of a
horse that
Natalie had
drawn on the red
plaster.

"Of course!" Mum and Doctor Sophie
both said at the same time.

"I thought you'd be pleased to get rid
of it!" the doctor laughed. "What's the
first thing you're going to do now that
you're better?"

Cara squealed with joy. "We're going to get a dog!"

"Oh, wow!" Doctor Sophie said. "That is exciting! Well, make sure you take it easy at first and don't run about after it too much – your leg is still a bit delicate. Remember, dogs have four legs, and you've only got two, so you've got to look after them!"

*

The next day Cara and her mum took the bus to Battersea Dogs & Cats Home. Cara's leg was still a bit sore and achy, but she was so excited she couldn't sit still! Finally they were nearly at the right stop and Mum told Cara to press the

button. Then they jumped off and walked until they got to the building where all the animals were carefully looked after. When Cara saw the big blue sign with the dog and cat curled up together she couldn't stop herself from jumping up and down!

When they went inside they were met by a nice lady called Mandy, who asked them all about their house. "It's only a little flat, but there is a garden," Mum said.

"With a trampoline and a climbing frame!" Cara told her.

"Gosh," Mandy smiled at Mum, "you must be quite active then."

"Oh yes!" Mum nodded her head. "Cara barely sits still for a second. In fact she recently broke her leg when she was racing around!"

Cara nodded and pointed to her right leg, wiggling her foot about. "It's fixed now but I've still got to 'take it easy'," she said, copying what Mum and Doctor Sophie had said to her over and over again.

Mandy laughed. "Well, funnily enough, we've got a puppy who recently broke *her* leg too. Would you like to meet her?"

"Well, we were looking for an older dog . . ." Mum started to say.

"Oh please, Mum!" Cara pleaded.

"The puppy broke her leg just like me!"

"All right then," Mum said, "but we're only going to look."

As they followed Mandy, Cara squeezed her mum's hand so hard that Mum had to tell her to stop – before *she* ended up with broken fingers!

Mandy took them over to a large cage with a very small black puppy inside.

Mandy called "Stella!" and the tiny dog turned round, showing Cara and Mum the white patch on her tummy.

"She is *so* cute!" Cara squealed. She bent down and put her fingers through the cage. "Hello, Stella!" she breathed. Stella trotted over to sniff Cara's hand, limping slightly on her front leg.

"She's a Staffie, do you know what that means?" Mandy asked Cara. Cara shook her head. "A Staffordshire Bull Terrier," Mandy explained, opening the door and letting Mum and Cara in to see Stella properly. "They're known for being really courageous and loyal dogs." The little puppy looked up at them and gave a grin, her tiny pink tongue poking out of her mouth.

"Her leg was broken when she arrived here with us," Mandy told them, "but our vet put it in a cast and it's better now. She's still got a limp but that will go away when her leg's fully healed."

"I didn't know dogs' legs mended just like ours!" Cara exclaimed as she bent down to stroke Stella's floppy ears. The tiny pup nuzzled into her palm, then rolled over so that Cara could stroke her white belly. Cara laughed. "Oh, she's gorgeous!" she cried.

Cara looked at her mum, who was gazing at Stella adoringly. "You hold her, Mum," Cara said, passing the wriggling puppy to her. Stella snuggled into Mum's arms and Mum squeezed her and stroked her velvety ears.

"Hello, Stella," Mum murmured. Cara held her breath. She knew Mum wanted an older dog, but it looked like she was falling in love with the tiny puppy. *Please, Mum*, Cara thought desperately. *Please love Stella as much as I do!*

Cara's Puppy

Cara held her breath. "Please can we have her, Mum?" she asked, crossing her fingers tightly.

"Well, she *is* gorgeous." Mum smiled, kissing the top of Stella's furry head. "And it's so funny that you both broke your legs at the same time. If you hadn't broken yours we might not be getting a dog now, and if Stella hadn't broken hers

we might not have come to see her. I
think we're *meant* to have her . . ."

Cara let out her breath in a rush, then
ran to give her mum an enormous hug,
being careful not to squash the tiny black
dog. "Oh thank you! Thank you!" Cara
squealed. Stella looked up at her with her
deep black eyes shining brightly. "Did
you hear that, Stella?" Cara whispered.
"You're *our*
puppy!"

*

The next week Mandy from Battersea
Dogs & Cats Home came round to Cara
and Mum's ground-floor flat to check
that it would be a
nice home for
Stella. Cara
showed her all
round the
garden and
gave her a
demonstration
on the trampoline.
At the end of her visit
Mandy told Cara and Mum that Stella
was definitely going to a good home, and
that they could come and pick her up
whenever they were ready.

"We'll have to borrow Grandpa's car so
we don't have to bring Stella home on

the bus," Mum told Cara, "but if it's OK
with Grandpa we can go and get Stella
tomorrow."

That night it felt like Christmas Eve.
Cara kept trying to go to sleep so that it
would be the next
day sooner, but
every time she
closed her
eyes she kept
imagining
Stella's
black face
and bright
beady eyes,
and
suddenly she
was wide
awake all over
again!

The next morning Cara and Mum took the bus to Grandpa's house and picked up his car, an old red Rover that Grandpa called the Mean Machine. Grandpa gave Cara a big hug and told her that he'd have to come round soon and meet Stella.

Cara was still tired from her sleepless night, and she must have fallen asleep in the car, because it only seemed like minutes before they were pulling up at Battersea Dogs & Cats Home.

"Come on, sleepyhead," Mum teased. "Let's go and pick up our puppy!"

When Stella saw them she leaped about barking excitedly. Mandy said goodbye to the little pup and passed her to Cara in the back of the car. Cara held Stella on her lap and waved to Mandy as they drove away, but Stella kept jumping up and trying to look out of the window.

"Hold her still," Mum said from the front. "She needs to sit safely in the car just like you do."

"She wants to see what's going on!" Cara said delightedly, holding Stella round her middle while she looked at everything they passed.

"There's Big Ben," she told her, pointing out the buildings as they went by. "And the London Eye. I went up there with Grandpa and I could see every single bit of London."

By the time they got home the little puppy looked completely worn out, and kept giving enormous puppy yawns.

"She's had a lot of excitement today," Mum said. "She's lived in Battersea Dogs & Cats Home for as long as she can remember, and now she's been all over London! Let's give her some supper and then she can have a snooze in her basket."

Mum went into the kitchen and opened a can of dog food. On the can it said it was rabbit and gravy, but when Cara looked inside it was just lots of brown lumps. Cara smelled it and wrinkled her nose in disgust. "Yuk!" she cried. "It's so stinky!"

"Well, Stella seems
to like the smell of
it," Mum laughed.
The puppy's tail
was wagging back
and forth so fast it was

almost a blur! Cara put Stella down on
the floor and poured food into the new,
blue dog bowl Mum had bought her,
using a fork to pull the food out of the
tin. The food tumbled
into the bowl, but
when it was put
on the floor,
Stella just
stared at it and
then looked up
and whined,
her big dark eyes
looking confused.

"It's for you, Stella," Cara said, stroking the little Staffie's soft, downy fur. Stella looked at her with a puzzled expression on her face.

"Perhaps it's a different type of food than she's used to," Mum wondered out loud.

"Come on, Stella." Cara knelt down next to the puppy and coaxed her. "Mmmm, yummy," she said, picking up one of the squidgy pieces and pretending to eat it. It still smelled horrid, but Cara didn't mind. She'd do anything to make sure that Stella ate.

She held it next to the little puppy's pink mouth. Stella sniffed it, then delicately nibbled at it, being careful not to bite Cara's fingers.

"That's it!" Cara cried, putting her hand closer to the bowl so that she led Stella to the rest of her dinner. Stella finished the first piece then put her nose into her bowl and gobbled the rest up

without hesitating.

"Well done, sweetheart," Mum said, ruffling Cara's hair.

"Well done, *Stella*!" Cara said, looking at the hungry dog.

Stella finished the last bit and limped over to curl up in Cara's lap. Cara stroked her and within minutes the little puppy was fast asleep!

Cara sat still on the kitchen floor while Stella slept, afraid to move in case she woke her up. As Mum bustled about making their dinner, Cara gently stroked the sleeping pup, running her fingers over Stella's black fur. Apart from the patch on her tummy Stella only had one other white bit, on her poorly front leg. It covered her foot and made her look like she was wearing a white sock on her paw. Cara was stroking the white paw, with its four little toes, when the phone rang.

Mum answered it and brought it into the kitchen, saying, "Cara, it's for you!"

Cara knew it would be Natalie. "Oh my gosh!" Natalie shrieked. "Have you got Stella yet?"

"She's sitting with me right now!" Cara replied, and Natalie squealed so loudly Cara had to pull the phone away from her ear before she was deafened! Stella's eyes popped open and she looked up at Cara and gave a doggy grin. "She is the most beautiful dog in the world," Cara said proudly, stroking the top of Stella's head.

"I really want to see her!" Natalie sighed.

"Come round for tea!" Cara told her, "you ask your mum and I'll ask mine."

"OK!" Natalie yelled excitedly.

Cara put the phone down and gently picked Stella up. "That was Natalie," Cara told the little puppy. "She's my best friend. Well, my best *human* friend, anyway," she added, stroking the pup under the chin. "Let's go and ask Mum if she can come round and meet you!" Still holding Stella, Cara rushed to find Mum and snuggled up next to her on the sofa.

"Mummy, please
can Natalie come
round and meet
Stella? Please
please please!"
Stella scrambled
over Cara's lap
onto Mum's and
looked up at her
pleadingly with her
chocolate-drop brown
eyes.

"All right," Mum
laughed, "as long as her mum says it's
OK."

Cara rushed over to the phone to call
Natalie back, but just as she got there it
rang. "Mum says I can come!" Natalie
said breathlessly.

"Yay!" Cara cried.

"Woof!" added Stella.

Natalie came straight round, and gasped when she saw Stella. "She is *so* gorgeous!" she squealed as she sat on the sofa next to the tiny dog. Cara felt really proud as she showed Stella off.

"Can I hold her?" Natalie asked, kneeling down to stroke the new puppy.

"Sure! I'll give you one of her doggy treats and you can hold her and feed her," Cara replied.

"Stella!" Natalie called. Stella started to run towards her, then turned and looked at Cara, as if to check it was OK.

"Go on!" Cara said with a smile. Stella bounded over to Natalie, who laughed happily and gave her a stroke.

"I love her!" she cried. "Oh, I wish I had a puppy!"

"You can come and visit her whenever you like," Cara told her kindly, "it'll be like she's yours too. And maybe you can ask for one for your birthday!"

"Oh! Can Stella come to my birthday party, Wendy?" Natalie asked Cara's mum. "It's in the garden, so she can run about."

"Stella and I will come and drop Cara off, but we might not stay," Mum told her. "She's still only a baby and she might be scared if there are too many people around."

"You'll love it, won't you,

Stella?" Cara said, skipping around the lounge with Stella chasing her heels.

"Ooh!" Natalie sighed, her eyes shining brightly. "This is going to be the best birthday ever!"

A Paw-fect Card!

A few days later, Cara woke up with a
start – there was something wet tickling
her face! She opened her eyes and saw a
tiny black face peering back at her. Cara
blinked and then grinned – Stella was
sitting on her and licking her nose!

"Woof!" Stella barked, as if to say "Oh
good, you're awake!" Her tail wagged
happily as Cara gave her a Good

Morning hug.

"Cara! Stella!" Mum called, and Stella leaped up and jumped off the bed. "Time to get up! Remember it's Natalie's birthday party today!"

Cara padded into the kitchen carrying Stella. Stella immediately started wriggling and as soon as Cara put her down she dived to her food bowl and started eating hungrily.

"She wouldn't touch her breakfast until you were awake!" Mum laughed, putting some toast in front of Cara.

"I think in the end she got a bit impatient and decided to wake you up herself."

After breakfast Mum told Cara to wrap up Natalie's present, which was a cuddly toy horse that Cara had picked out herself. "Can I make Natalie a card too?" Cara asked.

"OK," Mum grinned, "just make sure you don't make too much mess!"

Cara went and got her art things from under her bed. Stella crawled under too until all Cara could see was her tail.

"Come out of there, you funny pup!"
Cara giggled. She found some pretty
coloured paper and paints and grabbed
the animal magazines that were neatly
stacked up by her bed. "Natalie loves
horses as much as I love dogs," she told
Stella. "We can cut some pictures out of
the magazines
to decorate
her card!"
    Then
Cara had
an idea.
She folded
a piece of
blue card in half
and stuck a picture of a
Staffie puppy on the front
with glue. "Look, Stella!" she laughed.
"You've got a card to give Natalie too!"

Stella cocked her head to one side and studied it, then gave a bark of approval.

"Oh, lovely!" Mum smiled when she saw the cards. Cara had covered hers with pictures of horses and written 'HAPPY BIRTHDAY NATALIE' on the front in bright pink letters. Stella's had the dog picture and 'WOOF WOOF WOOF' written underneath. "That means 'Happy Birthday' in puppy-speak, doesn't it, Stella?" Cara said.

"Woof," Stella agreed.

"Beautiful," Mum declared. "But Stella needs to sign hers! Where are your paints?"

Cara rushed to get the box. Mum picked out one of Cara's finger paints and unscrewed the lid. "This is safe to use on your fingers so it's OK for Stella's paws as well."

Stella was nosing around the paints, sniffing about to see what was happening. Mum gently picked her up and dipped her paw into the top of the paint pot.

Then she held the wriggly puppy while
Cara carefully pressed her paw down on
the page. When she lifted Stella's leg up
Cara gasped in delight. There on the
page was a perfect little paw print! "Oh
Stella, Natalie's going
to love it!" she
cried. "Thanks,
Mum!"

"That's OK,"
Mum smiled.

"Just help me wash Stella's paw before she makes paint paw prints all over my carpet!"

Cara giggled and took Stella out of Mum's arms. Then she went over to the sink and turned the tap on. When the water was warm she washed Stella's paw until it was its usual pale pink colour.

"Now you're all ready for the party!" Cara joked, kissing the top of Stella's soft head. "And I need to get ready too!" Cara rushed into her room and pulled on her clothes.

When she walked into the kitchen with
Stella jumping round her ankles, Mum
sighed. "Can't you wear a pretty dress or
something? You're going to a birthday
party, not to work on a
farm!"

Cara looked
down at her
blue
dungarees.
"But there's
going to be a
bouncy
castle!" she
said, screwing
up her face. "I
won't be able to do
proper jumping if I'm wearing a *dress*."

As Mum shook her head Stella rushed
past and stood at the front door. Her tail

was wagging fiercely and she had a big doggy grin. "She knows we're going for a walk!" Cara said, and Stella's ears pricked up at the word.

"Woof!" she barked happily.

Natalie's Party

Cara bent down and clipped Stella's
bright pink lead onto her collar. Stella
jumped about excitedly, pulling on the
lead with her teeth, impatient to go. As
they set out it suddenly started to rain.
"Uh oh!" Cara cried, putting Natalie's
present under her jumper to keep it dry.
Stella was sniffing about excitedly,
barking at the falling raindrops and

snapping at them as they splashed into the puddles.

"I think we'd better catch the bus," Mum called, holding her handbag over her head to keep her hair dry.

"But what about Stella?" Cara said worriedly.

"She'll have to run along behind,"
Mum replied. Cara looked at her in
horror. When Mum saw her stricken face
she laughed out loud. "I'm only joking,
sweetheart!"

"But are dogs even allowed on buses?"
Cara asked.

"Yes, as long as they're well behaved,"
Mum told her.

Just then a bus sped
past, sending a
wave of puddle
water spraying
up over
them.

"Quick!" Mum yelled, chasing after it.
"That's our bus!"

"Come on, Stella, come on!" Cara
shouted. Stella ran alongside
Cara as they followed
Mum and jumped
on the bus.

Cara
held Stella's lead
up as the puppy jumped
on board, then praised her for being
such a good dog. Mum swiped their
passes and they went and sat down.
Stella sat on Cara's lap, looking out of
the window at the rainy street outside.

"Phew!" Mum sighed as she sat down next to them. The old gentleman opposite was already making a fuss of Stella, tickling her under her chin. The puppy was enjoying the attention and wriggled on Cara's lap so that the gentleman could tickle her white tummy. The old man chuckled and Mum laughed too.

"Don't spoil her too much or she won't want to get off!" Mum joked.

Cara smiled and rubbed her leg, which ached a bit. "Sorry, sweetheart, I shouldn't have made you run," Mum apologized.

"It's OK!" Cara said. "It's getting better – and it's definitely well enough to jump on the bouncy castle."

"If it doesn't stop raining soon I don't think there will *be* a bouncy castle," Mum replied.

Luckily, by the time they got to
Natalie's house the sun had come out,
and everyone was already gathered in
the back garden. The bouncy castle was
up and there was a big tent and a
table full of party food and
presents.

Mum stood back with Stella at first, while Cara ran to say hi to her friends and give Natalie her birthday present. Stella was looking round curiously, but she didn't seem a bit frightened by all the children.

"Mum, can Stella give Natalie her card?" Cara called. Mum nodded and let Stella off her lead. Stella shot over to Cara and covered her in licks as if she hadn't seen her in ages!

Natalie
loved her
cards, and
everyone
admired the
one from Stella
most of all.

Stella had a brilliant
time at the party being petted by all
Natalie's friends, but she was always
looking over to make sure that Cara was
OK. Once, when Cara was on the bouncy
castle Stella scrambled up
with her and looked
very surprised
that the floor
was moving
about!

When Natalie's mum brought out her
birthday cake – which was in the shape
of a galloping horse – everyone sang
Happy Birthday, and Stella joined in with

a howl. Everyone laughed, and Cara
scooped Stella up for a hug.

"I love you, Stella!" she whispered into
her fur.

Stowaway Stella

The next day Cara got up with a groan. It was Monday. Cara normally loved going to school, but she didn't want to spend the whole day without Stella!

"I wish Stella could come to school with me," Cara whined to Mum as she ate her breakfast.

"Well, she can't stay all day, but if we leave a bit earlier she and I could walk you there," Mum offered. "And we'll be there to pick you up as well. Then you get to see her – and me! – as soon as you finish school."

"Thanks, Mum!" Cara said, giving her a quick hug round her middle and then rushing off to put her school shoes on. Soon they were walking along, Stella pulling on her lead so that she could sniff all the interesting smells along the way. Mum and Cara were giggling about how excited the little dog was when a bus shot past them.

"Woof!" barked Stella, and started to run, her stocky legs moving quickly. She went so fast that she pulled her head right out of her collar, and Cara was left with the lead and collar – but no puppy!

"Stella!"
Cara called, running
after her. The little puppy
looked back and woofed again, as if to say *hurry up!* Mum and Cara were both running now, but they couldn't catch up.

Cara started to feel really worried. "Stella, come back!" she yelled. She went as fast as she could, but her leg was aching and slowing her down. Cara watched in alarm as Stella reached the bus and with one big leap jumped inside, looking back at them with a big grin.

"Stella!" Cara shouted, her voice high and panicky. "Get off!" But it was too late. The bus driver, high up in his seat, hadn't noticed the little stowaway on board. The doors closed, and Cara could see Stella's face peering through the glass, suddenly looking sad that Cara wasn't with her. Cara ran as fast as she could, but the bus was already pulling away.

Cara crumpled on the floor. Mum ran past, panting, but it was no use. She came back to Cara, who was crying huge gulping sobs. Cara clung on to Mum and cried and cried and cried. "She's only a baby and she's all on her own," Cara wailed, remembering the puppy's sad, confused little face. What if she never saw her again?

"We'll get her back," Mum said firmly.

She squeezed Cara extra tight. "I promise you. She'll most likely jump out at the next stop and come running straight back to us." Mum pulled Cara to her feet. "Come on, let's keep walking, she'll probably be just up ahead."

They carried on down the road, walking as fast as they could.

Cara's leg still hurt and she was limping a bit, but she ignored the ache and kept her eyes focused on the pavement ahead, anxiously looking out for a flash of black fur. But there was no sign of her puppy.

When they got to the school gates
Mum steered Cara
inside and came in
to speak to Mrs
Barnes to tell her
what had
happened. Her
voice sounded a
bit shaky when
she said, "We've
just lost our
puppy."

Mum reached
down to give Cara one
more hug. "I'll call the bus people and
they can radio the driver. Don't worry –
concentrate on school and Stella will be
here to pick you up at the end of the day.
OK?"

"OK." Cara sniffed.

Mum rushed away and Mrs Barnes took Cara into class. "Don't worry," she said kindly, "your mum will find your puppy in no time."

Natalie rushed over to give Cara a hug, making her sob again. Her tummy was tied up in knots and all she wanted to do was cry. "Stella will be OK," Natalie said in a small voice.

The day seemed to last forever and all Cara could think about was Stella. When the final bell went Cara shot out of her seat and into the playground. Mum was in her usual spot under the willow tree . . . but there was no puppy at her feet. Cara stopped and burst into tears.

Mum hadn't got her. Maybe Stella was lost for ever?

Mum rushed over. "I've found her!" she called quickly. "Stella's safe."

"Then where is she?" Cara gulped. "Doesn't she want to live with us any more? Did she run away because she doesn't love me?"

"No! No, sweetheart, she just saw the bus and got a bit over-excited, that's all," Mum said, stroking Cara's back soothingly. "The driver found her hiding under one of the seats at the end of his shift and,

realizing she was lost, took her to an
animal rescue centre.
And which one do
you think it
was? Battersea
Dogs & Cats
Home!
Battersea had
put a little
information
chip called a
microchip under
her fur so that
when the vet scanned it
they could see that she belongs to us."

"So where is she?" Cara cried.

"She's still at Battersea, they only
called a little while ago. I told them I'd
pick you up and we'd go there straight
from school."

Cara spent the whole journey with a funny mix of feelings. She was so happy that Stella was OK, but she wouldn't really believe it until she was holding the little puppy in her arms. And now she knew Stella was safe she was starting to feel cross with her for running away and making her have a horrible day being so worried. And she was so anxious to see Stella that she felt like she might cry all over again from happiness!

When they got to Battersea, Mandy was there to meet them. "Stella is through here," she said kindly.

She took them to
the pens and
there, curled up
and looking
very, very
sad, was the
small black
pup.

"Stella!"
Mandy called
out, "Cara's here."
At the word 'Cara' Stella looked up, and
when she saw Cara she
gave a happy bark
and rushed
forward, her tail
wagging wildly.
"WOOF!" she
barked, leaping
up at the cage.

Mandy
opened the door
and Stella flew
into Cara's
arms, licking
her face and
every part of
her she could
reach.

"Stella, I
was SO
WORRIED!" Cara
cried, hugging and
stroking the excited
puppy. "You must never run
away ever again!"

Stella nuzzled even closer and gave a
muffled woof. She was so happy to see
Cara that her tail kept wagging even
though she was being told off.

"I think she's learned her lesson," said
Mum, stroking Stella's ears. Stella looked
up and licked Cara on the tip of her nose.
"Woof!" she said, and snuggled in
Cara's arms – right where she belonged.

Read on for lots more . . .

Battersea Dogs & Cats Home

Battersea Dogs & Cats Home is a charity that aims never to turn away a dog or cat in need of our help. We reunite lost dogs and cats with their owners; when we can't do this, we care for them until new homes can be found for them; and we educate the public about responsible pet ownership. Every year the Home takes in around 12,000 dogs and cats. In addition to the site in south-west London, the Home also has two other centres based at Old Windsor, Berkshire, and Brands Hatch, Kent.

The original site in Holloway

History

The Temporary Home for Lost and
Starving Dogs was originally opened in a
stable yard in Holloway in 1860 by Mary
Tealby after she found a starving puppy
in the street. There was no one to look
after him, so she took him home and
nursed him back to health. She was so
worried about the other dogs wandering
the streets that she opened the Temporary
Home for Lost and Starving Dogs. The
Home was established to help to look
after them all and find them new homes.

Sadly Mary Tealby died in 1865, aged
sixty-four, and little more is known about
her, but her good work was continued. In
1871 the Home moved to its present site
in Battersea, and was renamed the Dogs'
Home Battersea.

Some important dates for the Home:

1883 – Battersea start taking in cats.

1914 – 100 sledge dogs are housed at the Hackbridge site, in preparation for Ernest Shackleton's second Antarctic expedition.

1956 – Queen Elizabeth II becomes patron of the Home.

2004 – Red the Lurcher's night-time antics become world famous when he is caught on camera regularly escaping from his kennel and liberating his canine chums for midnight feasts.

2007 – The BBC broadcast *Animal Rescue Live* from the Home for three weeks from mid-July to early August.

Amy Watson

Amy Watson has been working at
Battersea Dogs & Cats Home for six years
and has been the Home's Education
Officer for two and a half years. Amy's
role means that she organizes all the
school visits to the Home for children
aged sixteen and under, and regularly
visits schools around Battersea's three

sites to teach children how to behave and stay safe around dogs and cats, and all about responsible dog and cat ownership. She also regularly features on the Battersea website – www.battersea.org.uk – giving tips and advice on how to train your dog or cat under the "Amy's Answers" section.

On most school visits Amy can take a dog with her, so she is normally accompanied by her beautiful ex-Battersea dog Hattie. Hattie has been living with Amy for just over a year and really enjoys meeting new children and helping Amy with her work.

The process for re-homing a dog or a cat

When a lost dog or cat arrives, Battersea's Lost Dogs & Cats Line works hard to try to find the animal's owners. If, after seven days, they have not been able to reunite them, the search for a new home can begin.

The Home works hard to find caring, permanent new homes for all the lost and unwanted dogs and cats.

Dogs and cats have their own characters and so staff at the Home will spend time getting to know every dog and cat. This helps decide the type of home the dog or cat needs.

There are five stages of the re-homing process at Battersea Dogs & Cats Home. Battersea's re-homing team wants to find you the perfect pet, sometimes this can take a while, so please be patient while we search for your new friend!

1 Application

2 Interview

3 Home visit

4 Searching for a pet

5 Leaving with your new pet

Have a look at our website:
http://www.battersea.org.uk/dogs/ rehoming/index.html for more details!

"Did you know?" questions about dogs and cats

- Puppies do not open their eyes until they are about two weeks old.

- According to *The Guinness Book of Records*, the smallest living dog is a long-haired Chihuahua called Danka Kordak from Slovakia, who is 13.8cm tall and 18.8cm long.

- Dalmatians, with all those cute black spots, are actually born white.

- The greyhound is the fastest dog on earth. They can reach speeds of up to 45 miles per hour.

- The first living creature sent into space was a female dog named Laika.

- Cats spend 15% of their day grooming themselves and a massive 70% of their day sleeping.

- Cats see six times better in the dark than we do.

- A cat's tail helps it to balance when it is on the move – especially when it is jumping.

- The cat, giraffe and camel are the only animals that walk by moving both their left feet, then both their right feet, when walking.

Dos and Don'ts of looking after dogs and cats

Dogs dos and don'ts

DO
- Be gentle and quiet around dogs at all times – treat them how you would like to be treated.
- Have respect for dogs.

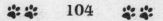

DON'T
- Sneak up on a dog – you could scare them.
- Tease a dog – it's not fair.
- Stare at a dog – dogs can find this scary.
- Disturb a dog who is sleeping or eating.

- Assume a dog wants to play with you. Just like you, sometimes they may want to be left alone.
- Approach a dog who is without an owner as you won't know if the dog is friendly or not.

Cats dos and don'ts

DO
- Be gentle and quiet around cats at all times.
- Have respect for cats.
- Let a cat approach you in their own time.

DON'T
- Never stare at a cat as they can find this intimidating.

- Tease a cat – it's not fair.
- Disturb a sleeping or eating cat – they may not want attention or to play.
- Assume a cat will always want to play. Like you, sometimes they want to be left alone.

Here is a delicious recipe for you to follow.

Remember to ask an adult to help you.

Cheddar Cheese Dog Cookies

You will need:

227g grated Cheddar cheese

(use at room temperature)

114g margarine

1 egg

1 clove of garlic (crushed)

172g wholewheat flour

30g wheatgerm

1 teaspoon salt

30ml milk

Preheat the oven to 375°F/190°C/gas mark 5.

Cream the cheese and margarine together. When smooth, add the egg and garlic and mix well. Add the flour, wheatgerm and salt. Mix well until a dough forms. Add the milk and mix again.

Chill the mixture in the fridge for one hour.

Roll the dough onto a floured surface until it is about 4cm thick. Use cookie cutters to cut out shapes.

Bake on an ungreased baking tray for 15–18 minutes.

Cool to room temperature and store in an airtight container in the fridge.

Some fun pet-themed puzzles!

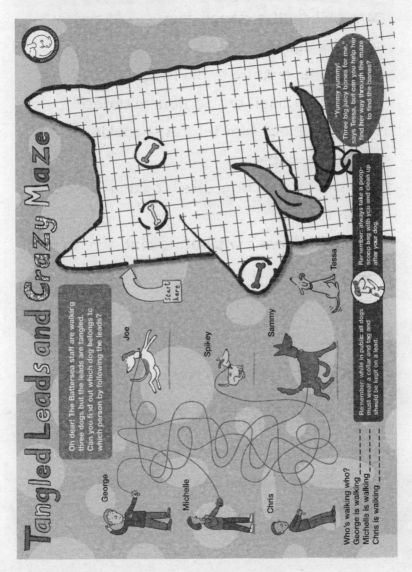

Here is a list of things that you need to think about before getting a dog. See if you can find them in the word search and while you look, think why they might be so important. Only look for words written in black. They can be written backwards, diagonally, forwards, up and down, so look carefully and GOOD LUCK!

SIZE
MALE OR FEMALE
AGE
COAT TYPE
COST
BEHAVIOUR
BASIC TRAINING
HOUSE TRAINING
TIME ALONE
GOOD WITH: PETS, CHILDREN,
STRANGERS, DOGS
HOW: ENERGETIC, CUDDLY,
STRONG WILLED, INDEPENDENT

Remember: when training a dog, reward works better than punishment.

Can you think of any other things? Write them in the spaces below.

```
I N D E P E N D E N T U N O P M S D H W
S X C V B N H R D G H I L J A N E V X Q
F T I M E A L O N E N M K E R Q U S P
G T H S W V B J P X Z D F E H I Y J T M
A C V B O M G D F D S C T Y A A O P R W
F R O U Z C H I L D R E N C Y L I O A K
G D V B I D F J L Q W E V Z L C O Z N R
T G H Y J K L H M N F D S E R T J N G P
M U I L D F G O H K V M F E T Y J K E M
A G H D N C V U B C V P O G M T R I R O
L W X D Z V G S I N E B F C E X P Z S I
E T Q U A D B E H D L N K Y A G E J G L
O R J C O A T T Y P E N U F D G Z S G L
F O R X A O K A Q E N S N M Y I E Q Z L
E N E R G E T I C P A S V F H B N H X K
M W D F B V H N L K G R U O I V A H E B
A S Q E T R Y I D A C X B U K O Y T F C
L Q D S T R O N G W I L L E D N J M X Z
E H G V N H K G N I N I A R T C I S A B
```

Dog Breeds Crossword

Across

2 A breed used as police dogs and sometimes called an Alsatian. (6,8)

5 A dog that is a mixture of breeds. (7)

6 A breed commonly used as guide dogs for the blind. (8)

9 Smallest breed of dog. (9)

11 A brown/liver and white breed often referred to as sniffer dogs. (8,7)

14 A French breed with very curly hair, traditionally used as a gun dog. (6)

15 A small black and tan terrier that was used to catch rats. (6)

16 A small white terrier from Scotland. (6)

17 A small breed with short legs and a long back, sometimes called a sausage dog. (9)

18 The dog often used as the symbol of Great Britain. (7)

Down

1 A spotted dog from a Disney film that needs lots of walking as a pet. (9)

3 A breed associated with a brand of paint. (3,7,8)

4 This breed is used to herd sheep and needs lots of activity such as agility if kept as a pet. (6,6)

7 Eddie from the programme *Frasier* is one of these. (11)

8 A breed associated with a brand of shoes. (6,5)

10 Scooby Doo was one of these very large dogs. (5)

12 These dogs are used for racing but also make good pets. (9)

13 Smaller version of 'Lassie' dog. (7)

Help!
Al is trying to count the dogs but some of them keep running about.
How many can you count?

Remember: all dogs need exercise in order to keep them fit and healthy and to give mental stimulation.

There are lots of fun things on the website, including an online quiz, e-cards, colouring sheets and recipes for making dog and cat treats.

www.battersea.org.uk